MW00955393

TREASURES IN THE WINDOW

The Seashell's Message

SHIRLEY J. LICHTY

ISBN 978-1-63903-708-7 (paperback)
ISBN 978-1-63903-709-4 (digital)

Copyright © 2023 by Shirley J. Lichty

All rights reserved. No part of this publication may be reproduced, distributed, or transmitted in any form or by any means, including photocopying, recording, or other electronic or mechanical methods without the prior written permission of the publisher. For permission requests, solicit the publisher via the address below.

Christian Faith Publishing
832 Park Avenue
Meadville, PA 16335
www.christianfaithpublishing.com

Printed in the United States of America

CONTENTS

1

CHAPTER 1

Getting Ready

Sage opened her eyes as she looked toward the window from her bed. It was very early, but this was the day she and Sam were waiting for. Sage could hear her mother's voice from downstairs. She needed to get up and get dressed. Pushing her blankets aside, Sage walked around her bed to the bright red suitcase on the floor. The zipper on the suitcase was closed. *I don't want to forget anything,* she thought, opening her suitcase for one more look inside. A new swimsuit and her favorite sundress were on top. A pink sun hat with seashell designs was in a special side pocket.

The bedroom door opened, and Sage turned to see who it was.

"Sage," said Sam. "Are you ready to go? Dad is packing the car." Sam was already dressed in blue shorts and a white T-shirt with a large whale printed on it. Whales were Sam's favorite animal.

"I'm not ready yet," replied Sage. "Go tell Mom I'll be down in a minute."

Sage looked back at the stack of neatly folded clothes.

"Sam, check our list to be sure we have everything."

"Okay!" said Sam as he hurried out of the room. Sam and Sage made a list of all the things they wanted to bring on the trip.

She could hear Sam running down the stairs.

"Sage will be down in a minute," said Sam in an excited voice.

"Good," replied their mother. Now Sage could hear her father's voice. That must mean that he is almost done packing the car.

Every summer, their family would go to Seabird Island. It was a long trip, but Sage did not care. She and Sam loved the beach. They would play in the warm powdery sand, run through the foaming waves, and go fishing with their father off the long pier. The best part of their vacation was visiting Aunt Lacey and Uncle Jonah.

Aunt Lacey and Uncle Jonah have a seashell shop on the main street of the island. The shop is filled with amazing creations from the ocean. There are seashells of every color, shape, and size. Sage would spend each morning helping Aunt Lacey in the shop. Sam liked to watch Uncle Jonah build models of tall sailing ships.

Uncle Jonah would tell stories about old fishing boats at sea, sunken treasure, and fish living deep below the waves. Their favorite story was about the old treasure chest in the shop window.

Uncle Jonah was working on his boat at the dock when a stranger approached him. His clothes were old and torn, and his boat was in need of repair. Uncle Jonah helped the fisherman fix his boat and gave him some clean clothes. In return, the fisherman gave Uncle Jonah a mysterious old trunk. Aunt Lacey thought the trunk looked like a treasure chest. They placed it in the shop window, and that's how Treasure Chest Seashell Shop got its name.

Sage hurried to get dressed. Quickly, she closed and zipped her suitcase. The shorts and shirt she planned to wear were on the chair beside her bed. The fabric covering the chair was soft like velvet. Sometimes, Sage would sit there and read until she fell asleep.

Beside the chair was a shelf full of books. Sage loved to read. There were books about famous people and stories about children who lived in other countries. There were books about oceans, deserts, and places where it was very cold. Her favorite books to read were those on space travel and the planets. Her father was a scientist who worked at the space center. She and Sam had been there many times.

"Are you almost ready, Sage?" said her mother from the hallway.

"Yes, almost," answered Sage as she brushed her hair in front of the round mirror on the wall above the shelf of books. In the mirror, she could see the reflection of her favorite doll. "I almost forgot her." Sage turned and reached across the bed, gently placing her fingers around the doll's tiny arm.

The doll was from a shop in Paris. It was a gift from Major Marsley. Major Marsley was in the astronaut training program at the space center. She was always traveling to different countries. Now, she was part of the crew selected to travel in the newest fastest space vehicle. Someday, Sage would train to be an astronaut. There were many jobs at the space center, but going into space was her dream.

CHAPTER 2

The Birthday Box

Sage remembered the day Major Marsley gave her the doll. It was the day they had the big birthday party for her father. Aunt Lacey and Uncle Jonah were there. Several people from the space center were there also. It was a very large place. Their father worked in a building where they designed robots to use in space travel and to explore faraway planets. Sometimes, their father would ask them to choose a name for the robots, and they would think of the funniest names.

It was a sunny day, and everyone was outside on the deck. There were birthday balloons shaped like planets and rockets suspended from the deck railings. One of the rockets took off traveling high in the sky. In a few seconds, it drifted out of sight.

Meanwhile, Sam was in the backyard tossing a ball to their dog, Annie. Annie chased the ball and brought it back to Sam.

"Come up, Sam," called their mother. Sam and Annie quickly came up the deck steps and joined the party. There was one large box and lots of smaller gifts scattered across the top of the picnic table. The lid on the large box had several holes in it. Aunt Lacey, Mom, and Major

Marsley were looking at the large box and quietly talking. *I wonder why there are holes in the box*, thought Sage.

"Well, I better see what is inside this box," said their father as he got up from his chair. He removed the lid and looked inside. "So who is this?" said their father with a big smile.

"We named him *Albert*," said one of the men.

"He has been roaming around the hangar while we're working on the new spacecraft. He is sleeping in the hangar at night, so we don't think he has a home. It's going to get dangerous for him when we start firing up the super engines," said the man wearing a ball cap and sunglasses. "It is not good to have a cat around powerful computer equipment and astro-robots."

When it got quiet, Albert poked his head out of the box. Up he went like a rocket landing on the table. He was not a tiny kitty but tall and thin. Narrow orange stripes covered his back and sides. Quickly, he walked to the edge of the table and looked down to the deck floor. Looking up again, he glanced around the deck as if he had to make a decision. Suddenly, he leaped off the table, down the deck steps, and under a small spruce tree at the corner of the house.

Sage glanced at her mother's face, but she did not appear surprised. Major Marsley must have told her about the cat before the party. She followed her mother inside the house to get the birthday cake.

It was an amazing cake covered with smooth dark chocolate frosting. Drops of creamy vanilla stars were spaced evenly over the top. Their mother called it the Milky Way cake. Sage helped to place the tiny rocket-shaped wax candles into the soft frosting. The man with the ball cap and sunglasses reached over to light the candles. As each candle was lit, it made a crackling sound as if the tiny rockets were blasting off. Uncle Jonah began to sing "Happy Birthday," and everyone joined in.

Albert was a great birthday cat. He followed Sage and Sam everywhere. Even Annie made friends with him right away.

As the days went by, everyone began to realize that Albert was not a regular-thinking cat. He was a lovable cat, but he could do a lot of amazing things. Albert could read. Not out loud, but in a way that a cat like Albert could do. He would read only what he wanted to read. He could press the buttons on a calculator with his paw and add numbers in the millions. When their father and Albert played Chess, their father would say it was a long and difficult game. Albert could even place his paw on the correct card and win every game. Sam would not let Albert play anymore.

No one could explain why Albert could do all these things. Their father thought Albert may have spent too much time watching the robots. Mom thought that he might have eaten something. Sam thought it was good that Albert had a home with real people and not robots. Sage did not know how a cat could know so much without going to school.

CHAPTER 3

"Thanks, Albert"

Sage looked down at her doll's round face and dark bouncy curls. A tiny button fastened the cherry-red cape and matching hat. Sage hoped that one day, she would go to France. But right now, she could not wait to get to Seabird Island.

Sage turned to take one quick look around the room to be sure she did not forget something. She went into the hallway, and there was Albert and Annie waiting for her. "Are you ready to go on a long trip?" said Sage, looking down with a smile. "Come on, let's go."

Albert and Annie quickly went in front of her and down the stairs. Annie went toward the front door, but Albert stopped at the bottom of the stairs.

"What is wrong, Albert?" said Sage. Albert went over to the brown leather chair by the window. On the seat of the chair was a piece of paper. It was the list of things she and Sam wanted to bring on the trip. Albert pushed the list off the chair with his paw, and placed the same paw on the words *card games*. Sage looked toward the shelf by the TV. There were the card games and the box of markers. "Thanks, Albert, we almost forgot them." She was sometimes amazed at what Albert could do.

Sage went to get a bag for the games and markers. She liked to draw. Her father always told her that she was a little artist.

"Let's hurry, Albert."

Annie remained at the front door. Her eyes followed Sage as she walked across the room. Annie must have been a very good service dog. She was a cheerful friendly Labrador retriever, with creamy-yellow fur. Annie had a gentle look, but she was quick to spot danger.

With her doll tucked under her arm, the handle of her suitcase in one hand, and the bag of games and markers in the other, Sage, Annie, and Albert went out the front door. "You have a lot of things there," said her father, reaching out to take her suitcase.

"Hurry up!" called Sam from his open window in the van.

"Are we ready to go?" asked their mother in a cheerful voice. Albert and Annie jumped in, and their father closed the door. As they drove out of the driveway, they passed the large leafy maple trees that lined their street.

It was a sunny morning, so Sage put on her sunglasses. She even had a tiny pair of stylish sunglasses for her doll to wear on the trip.

"We almost forgot the card games." Sage looked toward Sam as she spoke. "Albert told me."

Now her father responded. "He did?"

"Yes, he put his paw right on the words *card games*," replied Sage.

"It is hard to determine what Albert learned from being around the robots and the spacecraft computer. It just can't be measured," said their father.

"Albert certainly does some very unusual things," replied their mother. "Last week, I saw him on the kitchen counter. It looked like he was reading my chocolate chip cookie recipe."

"Do you think Albert could bake cookies?" asked Sam with a smile. They all laughed.

Annie made a little barking sound. "I think Annie agrees," responded Sage. "Remember when she came to live with us?"

"Yes," replied their mother. "Annie was a good service dog, but it was time for her to retire."

"I'm glad she came," Sam replied as he reached for a round container filled with green grapes. There were other containers filled with snacks for the trip.

Sage opened the bag and took out a matching game. "Let's play," said Sage.

"Okay," replied Sam. They played the game several times until they got tired.

It was night when they crossed the drawbridge to Seabird Island. The bridge was high above the water. The lights on the bridge were bright. When they drove off the bridge, the streets on the island were dark.

CHAPTER 4

The Cottage

When Sage opened her eyes, she saw the reflection of the sun on the yellow wall beside her bed. Every room in the cottage was a different beach-like color. Sage liked the bright colors. She could hear the sound of the ocean. Sage loved to hear that sound.

"Sage." It was Sam, looking up at her from the bottom bunk bed. Sam got up and ran out of the room. Sage climbed out of the top bunk. Annie spent the night in a dog bed in the corner of the room. Her eyes followed Sage as she came down the ladder. Albert appeared at the bedroom door. He slept on the porch curled up on the chair with the green palm print cushion.

Sam ran back into the bedroom. "Mom and Dad are making breakfast." Sage could smell the bacon frying. "I can't wait to put my swimsuit on and go out on the sand," said Sam in an excited voice.

After breakfast, everyone got ready to go outside. The cottage was on stilts high off the ground. Sage, Sam, Albert, and Annie went out the back door and down the steep wooden stairs to the beach. Sage, Sam, and Annie walked onto the warm sand.

Albert stopped on the last step. He carefully placed one paw in the sand and quickly pulled it back. Albert could do many things, but stepping in the sand was one thing he would not do.

Their father was putting an umbrella into the sand. Back and forth, back and forth, he went, grasping the handle of the umbrella tightly with both hands. He stopped when the umbrella was firmly standing. A large, white cooler and a stack of beach chairs were a few feet from the umbrella.

Their mother was coming down the stairs with the beach towels and a large blue-and-white, striped blanket. Annie quickly ran under the umbrella. Albert was still on the last step. "Annie, move out of the way," said their mother as she placed the blanket down under the umbrella. "Go get Albert, Sam," said their mother.

Sam ran over to the steps and carried Albert to the blanket. Albert jumped out of Sam's grip and onto the blanket beside Annie.

15

Sage and Sam ran down to the water with their buckets. The ocean was a clear blue color, and seashells covered the wet sand. Sage looked for shells while Sam filled his bucket with water. Sam brought the water back to the edge of the blanket and worked on building a sandcastle. They played for a long time.

Sage returned to the blanket with several seashells in her bucket. "Look at this shell." Sage reached into the bucket and took out a shiny white seashell with a pearl-like glaze. The shell was curved, and the edges were smooth.

"That is a nice one," replied her mother, looking up at the shell Sage was holding in her hand.

"I think I'll keep that one," said Sage as she examined the other shells in the bucket.

CHAPTER 5

The Seagulls

The large waves made it hard to go out in the water. Sam was busy building a giant sandcastle. Sage went to help with the project.

"I am making a moat around the castle," said Sam.

"When we finish, let's take a walk," replied Sage. "Let's go before Aunt Lacey and Uncle Jonah come. They have to work at the shop until lunch."

"That's a great castle," said their mother as she took a picture of the sand creation.

"Can Sage and I take a walk?" asked Sam.

"You can only go as far as the hotel," said their mother. There were only a few people on the beach around them, but near the hotel, there were many more.

"I want a snack," said Sam.

"Take a small peanut butter sandwich," said their mother. Sam took a sandwich out of the cooler. Sage picked up Albert and gently touched the soft warm fur on Annie's head.

"Come on, Annie." Annie got up and walked between Sam and Sage. They walked along the edge of the water. The waves would come up and cover their feet.

Annie did know how to swim. She learned when she was a service dog. They saw Annie swim several times. Sage stopped to pick up seashells as the group walked along.

Sam was holding his sandwich and had only taken a few bites. Up ahead, they could see about ten seagulls standing in a row. They were looking for fish in the water. "I am going to give my sandwich to the seagulls. They look hungry." Before Sage could say anything, Sam threw his sandwich to the seagulls. It landed on the wet sand in front of the line. The seagulls rushed to get part of the treat. Sage and Sam stood and watched as each seagull tried to get their share.

One was able to grasp the entire sandwich in his beak. Instantly, he flew up into the sky over the ocean waves. Another seagull quickly went up after him. Now both seagulls had a grasp on the sandwich. Flying in circles, round and round they went, with their beak tightly closed around the bread. Suddenly, the sandwich fell down, down, down into the moving water. It disappeared in the ocean waves.

"Oh, no," said Sam. "There goes my sandwich into the water. None of the birds got to eat it."

"That's because the seagull wanted to eat the whole thing," Sage replied in a firm voice. "They didn't want to share."

The two seagulls flew back to the group. Some of the birds were squawking as if they were disappointed or even angry. Others remained in the line.

Suddenly, Albert leaped from Sage's arms and onto the wet sand. His body froze, and his eyes widened as if he saw a monster fish appear in the ocean.

Sage and Sam watched in horror as they saw Annie tossing helplessly in the waves. Her legs went up and down as the strong current pulled Annie into deeper water.

Albert did not move. He stood like a statue exactly where he landed. Albert began to shake his head back and forth as if he were trying to think of a way to help Annie.

Sage and Sam called out. "Annie, Annie!" Annie could not fight the powerful waves. She was just a little dog in a big ocean. Every wave was pulling her farther and farther away. Annie disappeared in the waves. She appeared again trying to paddle to the shore.

How did this happen? Was Annie trying to get the peanut butter sandwich for the seagulls? Annie was trained to help others, and now no one could help her.

Another wave was growing larger and larger in the distance. Sage started to walk out into the water. It was like she was one of the robots her dad designed. The water was getting deeper, and the waves would soon crash on her and pull her out. Sage was afraid. She could not go out any farther to save Annie. Sage moved back, keeping her eyes fixed on the struggling form.

Sage was just about to turn and run for help when she heard the screeching sound of the seagulls.

The seagulls were flying over Sage, Sam, and Albert and over the waves. There was Annie fighting to keep her head out of the water and trying to paddle toward them. Another big wave was heading

toward her. The seagulls flew over Annie. They turned around and flew toward her.

"What are they doing!" cried Sam.

"Annie! Annie!" shouted Sage as if to warn her.

Like a giant parachute coming down from the sky, the seagulls landed in the water behind Annie. They looked as if they were one large bird. Annie could not stop them. The seagulls did not make a sound. They lifted their feathers and joined together around Annie. She looked like a big gray cloud drifting away. Then like a powerful engine, the seagulls pushed Annie. The rolling waves moved the ball of feathers up and down. The dark tip of Annie's nose could be seen pointing toward the shore. Annie's eyes were fixed on the three figures standing in the distance. Closer and closer, she came with her fur covered in feathers. She continued to paddle as the seagulls pushed her to safety. When Annie's paws could touch the sandy bottom, she leaped out of the water just as a large wave broke behind her. Making lots of noise, the seagulls flew off together in a line over the crashing waves.

Annie ran straight to Sage, Sam, and Albert. Sage dropped her bucket of shells and threw her arms around Annie's wet fur. She could feel Annie shaking. "It's okay, Annie. You are safe now." Albert gently placed his paw on Annie's paw. Sam knelt down and looked at Annie with a relieved face. Sam did not say anything.

The happy group began to walk back. In the distance, they could see Aunt Lacey and Uncle Jonah walking toward them. Sam ran ahead, and Aunt Lacey gave him a hug. "Did Annie take a swim?" asked Uncle Jonah. Sam began to tell the story.

"Do you think Annie was trying to get the sandwich for the seagulls?" Sam looked up at Uncle Jonah for his answer. "Annie has been trained to be a service dog. She would do a lot to help anyone, even a seagull."

Uncle Jonah paused for a minute. "Do you know how Seabird Island got its name?" Sage turned and looked up at Uncle Jonah and shook her head.

Sam responded, "No. How?"

"Many years ago, some young and inexperienced boys went out on a fishing boat. While they were fishing, the sea became rough, and the weather got stormy. The boat drifted far from shore. The boys spent the night trying to keep control of the boat. Pounding waves can cause a small boat to break apart or even capsize. In the morning, they saw two birds. The birds flew back and forth from the bow to the stern. It was as if they were trying to get the boys' attention. The boys decided to follow the birds. Many hours went by before they saw land in the distance. This is the beach where they came onshore."

"This island has some very unusual birds especially the seagulls," replied Sam. A large wave broke and the ocean came and covered their feet.

"Are you two going to help us in the shop?" said Aunt Lacey with a smile.

"Oh yes!" said Sage in an excited voice.

Uncle Jonah carried Albert as the group walked through the shallow waves and wet sand. The hot sun dried Annie's fur before they reached the umbrella.

"How was your walk?" called their father from his beach chair.

"You both must be thirsty. Come, sit under the umbrella," said their mother as she handed them each a bottle of cold water from the cooler. Sage gave Albert and Annie some water from a plastic container.

"Mom, I have to tell you what happened to Annie during our walk." Sage told her mother the whole story.

"Well, I am just happy that Annie is all right." Her mother leaned down from her chair to pat Annie's head.

"Aunt Lacey said we can work at the seashell shop again!" said Sage with an excited voice. "Can we?"

"Yes," said her mother.

"Yea!" responded Sam with a big smile.

CHAPTER 6

The Clipper Ship

At the end of a long day at the beach, they went to Aunt Lacey's house for dinner. After dinner, they all walked to the ice cream shop. The Happy Turtle Ice Cream Shop was on Main Street. They passed the post office and an art gallery. In the window of the gallery, there were paintings of a lighthouse by the ocean, dolphins jumping through the waves, and colorful umbrellas spread across the sandy beach.

"There's the Happy Turtle," Sam called out as he pointed to the sign at the end of the block. The group went inside the bright-green door of the shop. The walls were covered with turtle designs. The turtles were smiling, scooping, and eating ice cream. Even the napkin holders on each table were in the shape of a turtle shell.

"What flavor would you like?" said the lady behind the counter looking at Sam. Sam would always get the same flavor—chocolate chip. The lady put a big scoop of ice cream in a sugar cone and gave it to Sam. Sage had to think for a few minutes before she could make a decision.

"I want a fudge sundae with whipped cream and sprinkles," said Sage to her father as they stood in line.

After they finished eating their ice cream, Sage, her mother, and Aunt Lacey went back to the cottage.

"I want to show you one of the ships I am working on," said Uncle Jonah. Sam and his father went with Uncle Jonah to the shop. They walked to the back door. Sam watched as Uncle Jonah entered the code 3127 to open the door. "This is the largest ship I have ever made." As they entered the shop, the tall, white sails gleaned from the light of the opened door.

On a heavy oak table was a large model sailing ship. There were small cans of paint, tubes of glue, pieces of wood, white cloth and thread, and other tools to build the ships. Behind the table were shelves with smaller ships for people to buy. The walls in the room were filled with pictures of different types of boats and ships. Sam walked around the old oak table to see every side of the amazing ship.

"Sam, tomorrow we will work on this clipper ship," said Uncle Jonah., Sam stopped to have one more glimpse of the beautiful boat. "The Clipper is a fast sailing ship. The clipper could have as many as thirty-five sails. Long ago, it was used to carry cargo," explained Uncle Jonah.

"That's really interesting," said Sam's father as they left the shop.

CHAPTER 7

Helping in the Shop

After breakfast the next morning, Sage, Sam, Albert, and Annie headed to the seashell shop. They went out the porch door and down the steps onto the sandy road. On the other side of the street lived Mr. and Mrs. Duffy. They were very friendly. When the Duffys were sitting on their porch, they would wave and say hello. Mrs. Duffy always had hanging pots filled with pretty flowers. The Duffy's lived on the island for a long time. They also have a big black and white dog named Buddy. They would see Mr. Duffy walking Buddy in the evening.

There was no one staying in the house next to their cottage. A red golf cart was parked in the driveway under the house. Many of the homes on the island are built on stilts high off the ground. This protects them from water and waves during a storm.

Aunt Lacey and Uncle Jonah's cottage came next. It had a white picket fence decorating the front yard. A large palm tree stood between Aunt Lacey's house and the back door of the seashell shop.

They were almost on Main Street. The group turned the corner, and they were in front of Aunt Lacey's shop. The sign below the store window read *Treasure Chest Seashell Shop*. The shop was painted a pale blue with a white door and trim. In the shop window was the old treasure chest. Uncle Jonah told them about the fisherman who gave him the chest. It must have been on a ship that sank a long time ago. The trunk was covered with barnacles when the waves washed it up on the beach. The leather straps were worn, and the brass lock was broken and weathered. The trunk was empty except for some sand, seagrass, and pieces of broken shells. Uncle Jonah removed the barnacles and fixed the broken lock. The chest still looked old, but there was something special about it.

Sage and Sam ran into the shop. Aunt Lacey was unpacking boxes of new items to put on the shelves. "Good morning, children."

"Hi, Aunt Lacey," replied Sage. Sam walked closer to see what was inside.

"Hi," said Sam. "Where is Uncle Jonah? I want to help him build the ship."

"He is in the back of the shop ordering new things to sell," said Aunt Lacey. "There are a lot of things to take care of when you own a store." Sam quickly went down the aisle to see what Uncle Jonah was doing.

The shop was filled with gifts, toys, and items from the sea. There were large seashells and small ones. Seashells were on everything. There were scented candles with shells pressed into the wax, and pretty containers filled with seashells. In another aisle, there were lighthouse figures, colorful glass fish, and glittery ornaments. Shelves were filled with toys and items for children. There were stuffed fish, turtles, mermaids in sparkling outfits, and all types of toy boats.

Scattered throughout the shop were remote-controlled items with music, lights, and action.

"Can I help you?" said Sage.

"Yes," said Aunt Lacey. "Stack all of these boxes neatly on the bottom shelf."

Sage tried really hard to do a good job. She wanted to be a big help to Aunt Lacey. Sage especially liked it when Aunt Lacey asked her to help with the customers.

There were always new toys and items in the shop. This summer, some of the new toys and items played music and some would light up. Aunt Lacey only had a few operating during store hours.

Sage looked in the corner behind the checkout counter. There was Annie lying in her favorite spot. Albert was different. Sometimes, he was hard to find. Aunt Lacey had a bag of cat treats. When she shook the bag, Albert would come out of hiding.

Sage stayed busy all morning. Aunt Lacey gave her several jobs to do. One job was to place the cards and other items in a neat row. Another job was to place price tag stickers on the toys.

Sage noticed a new item in the shop. It was a treasure chest, but not like the one in the shop window. It was much smaller, and the gold lock on the front was bright and shiny. The top was painted with a pale-pink seashell design. When Sage opened the chest, she could smell the wood. *I hope no one buys it*, she thought.

The bell on the door rang, and Sage looked up. Her mother was coming into the shop. "Are you ready to go to the beach?" said her mother.

"Yes, I will get Sam."

In the back of the shop, Sam was helping Uncle Jonah unpack boxes of new items to sell. There was a desk in the corner of the room. A computer was on top of the desk. Albert was sitting in front of the screen. Sage walked closer to see what he was reading. There was a picture of seagulls flying over the beach. Below the picture were the words "The diet of a seagull." *They certainly like peanut butter sandwiches*, thought Sage.

"Albert is reading about seagulls," said Sam from the other side of the room.

"Mom is here, Sam." Sam got down off the stool.

"Can I help you tomorrow, Uncle Jonah?"

"Sure, have fun at the beach."

"Sage has been a big help this morning," said Aunt Lacey. "I think Albert and Annie will enjoy staying in the cool shop."

"Yes, that is a good idea," replied their mother. "Especially after yesterday's experience with the seagulls."

"Bye, Aunt Lacey," said Sage and Sam as they went out the shop door.

CHAPTER 8

The Whale

That night, Sage climbed up into the top bunk and placed her doll by the wall in her bed. She was just about to close her eyes when she heard Sam's voice. "Uncle Jonah gave me a toy whale, and I left it in the shop."

"You can get it tomorrow," whispered Sage.

"I really want it," said Sam in a sad voice.

"What do you want me to do?" whispered Sage in a firmer voice.

"Get it," said Sam.

"Do you mean go out in the dark?" asked Sage.

Now Sam put his face into the center of his pillow as he spoke. "Annie can come with us," replied Sam in a soft muffled voice. Sage moved to the edge of the bed and looked down at Sam, with his head still stuffed in the pillow. Sam turned his head to the side and again replied, "We can take Annie. She will protect us." This time, Sage knew exactly what Sam said. Annie lifted up her head when she heard her name.

"I know the key code," said Sam. He got out of bed and walked over to Annie. "I saw Uncle Jonah enter it when we went to the shop. Let's go!"

Sage did not want to go to the shop when Aunt Lacey and Uncle Jonah were not there. She reluctantly climbed down and put on her sandals. "Come on, Annie," whispered Sage.

Annie looked puzzled as she got up from her bed. Sage, Sam, and Annie went out the back door. Their sandals made a loud clacking sound as they went down the wooden steps. Sage could not wait until they were on the sandy road. "This is a bad idea," whispered Sage as they walked quickly in the dark.

The night air was warm. They could hear the ocean waves behind them as they walked toward the Main Street. They passed the Duffy's house. Sage hoped that Buddy would not start barking. Buddy would bark at any sound. He was a good watchdog.

Sage could see a dim light in the house with the red golf cart. *I'm glad no one is there now. What if someone sees us out here at night,* thought Sage.

They hurried past Aunt Lacey's house. The house was dark. The only light came from an old ship's lantern hanging by the porch door. Looking straight ahead, Sage could see the shadow of a car passing by on Main Street.

Sage felt safe since Annie was with them, but she did not like going into the shop with Sam at night. "Are you sure you really need the whale?" whispered Sage.

"Yes," said Sam in a louder voice.

"I can put the code in." Sam moved closer to the keypad. He entered the code, and the door opened. *I just wish Sam would have remembered the toy when he left the shop today*, thought Sage.

"Where is it?" said Sam as he looked around the back of the dark shop. He looked on the table where he and Uncle Jonah were working on a model ship that morning.

"I don't see it. Let's look up front," said Sage. Sam led the way to the small hallway toward the front of the shop.

"Wow!" cried out Sam in a surprised voice.

"What is going on?" exclaimed Sage. There were lights and music coming from every aisle. The shop was filled with sound and action. The toys were on and playing their song.

The man in the lighthouse was going in and out of the door, and the light was turning on the top. The toy turtle and crab were walking back and forth on the shelf, and the toy starfish was lit and playing music.

Annie growled at the toy crab as it scuttled across the floor. "What is happening?" said Sage.

"Did Aunt Lacey forget to turn off the toys?" said Sam.

"Aunt Lacey doesn't turn on these toys. She wouldn't want the crab and turtle walking around in the shop all night."

"There's my toy." Sam pointed to Annie coming from the front of the shop. Annie was carrying the toy whale in her mouth.

"Let's get out of here," said Sage. She did not feel right being in Aunt Lacey's shop at night. She did not like what was happening in the shop.

"I want to leave now," said Sage with a fearful voice.

"Come, Annie." They rushed out of the shop with Sam keeping a tight grip on the toy whale.

CHAPTER 9

The Secret

The next morning, Sage and Sam woke up to the sound of the screen door on the porch.

"I have some donuts from Jim's Bakery," said their father in a loud voice. Jim's Bakery was a few shops north on Main Street. Sam arrived at the porch table first.

"What type of donut do you want?" said their father. The box of donuts was opened. There were donuts covered with chocolate glaze and others with white powder. Some were filled with strawberry jelly dripping out the sides. There were donuts with no filling inside. Sam quickly reached into the box and grabbed a chocolate donut. Sage did not really care today. She just wanted to get to the shop.

"Can we go to the shop now?" said Sage as she took a small plain donut from the box.

"Are you feeling all right? said her mother in a concerned voice.

"Yes, I'm fine," said Sage.

"It is cloudy now, but it should be sunny soon," said their mother.

"Then we will go to the beach." Sam reached into the box to get another donut.

They went down the front steps and onto the sandy road to the Treasure Chest Seashell Shop.

"Hi, Uncle Jonah," they both said at the same time.

"Good morning," Uncle Jonah responded in a cheerful voice. Sam went over to the shelf where the toys had been walking the night before. The crab and the turtle were up on the shelf where they usually sat. Sam picked up the turtle and turned it over.

"This morning I found the turtle and crab on the floor," said Uncle Jonah. Sam looked down again at the turtle. "On or off?" asked Sam. Sam looked puzzled as he stared at the toy in his hand.

Uncle Jonah replied, "These toys run on a timer. After a few hours, they will turn off." Sam put the turtle back on the shelf.

"I am going to build a shelf to display some new items," said Uncle Jonah. Sage and Sam watched as he attached the pieces of wood. When one part of the shelf was connected, Uncle Jonah went to the back of the shop. He returned carrying the large model ship Sam had help build. Its white sails extended high over the misty blue hull. Uncle Jonah carefully moved down the narrow aisle toward the shop window. "Are you going to take the treasure chest out of the window?" asked Sam as he followed Uncle Jonah to the front of the shop. "No, I think this ship will look good beside the old trunk."

"What was inside the treasure chest, Uncle Jonah?" asked Sam looking at the big rectangular form.

"Before there were airplanes that could fly across the oceans, people traveled on ships," replied Uncle Jonah. "They used trunks like this to store their belongings. A trunk may have held someone's clothing, important papers, and other things they wanted to take with them. All the treasures they owned would be inside."

"Everything they owned would fit in there?" said Sam, looking up at the old trunk.

"It was a choice. To make the trip was a big decision. It's not like choosing what flavor of ice cream you want at the Happy Turtle. A big decision requires lots of prayer," replied Uncle Jonah.

Sage listened to Uncle Jonah's answer. Her thoughts went back to last night in the shop. How could she tell Uncle Jonah about the walking toys? She couldn't say that she and Sam were in the shop last night, looking for the toy whale.

Aunt Lacey walked in with some envelopes. "Here is the mail, Jonah," said Aunt Lacey. "Sage, I have a job for you and Sam today." Aunt Lacey went in the back room and came out carrying a large box with words printed all over the sides. She placed the box at the end of the counter.

Sage and Sam went to see what was in the box. Sam was not tall enough to see inside, so he quickly ran to get a stool. Aunt Lacey lifted the flaps of the box. Sage and Sam looked inside. The box was filled with tiny seashells. The shells were different colors and shapes. Some were curled and others were flat.

"I want you to put ten shells in each bag," explained Aunt Lacey. "Put a sticker on each bag and tie it closed." Aunt Lacey gave Sage a ball of silver string. Sage liked this job. She almost forgot about going into the shop at night.

Sage and Sam worked putting the tiny shells into bags. Sam counted the shells, and Sage tied the nicest bow she could do.

40

"Aunt Lacey, who lived in these shells?" asked Sage as she reached for a piece of string.

"Sea animals like clams, snails, and oysters. They need protection, so they make their own home or shell. The animals use salt and chemicals from the water, and add their own ingredients to form layers of shell. As the animal grows, it does not leave its shell. It makes a bigger shell."

"Like us," said Sam.

"Yes, something like that. But as we grow on the outside, we want to grow on the inside," replied Aunt Lacey.

Sage listened as she tied the last bag closed. "We need more bags, Aunt Lacey," said Sam. There were only a few more shells at the bottom of the box.

"You both did such a good job. You may have the rest of the shells."

Suddenly, Sage had an idea. "May I have this small piece of wood, Uncle Jonah?"

"Sure, that piece is not long enough for the shelves," replied Uncle Jonah as he placed a container of seashells and colorful beads on the top shelf.

Sage took a marker from the counter and began to draw. She drew a turtle, a starfish, and a flower on the wood. She arranged the tiny shells on the wood. It took a small amount of glue to keep the shells in place, and her picture was complete.

"Sage, that is a very pretty picture," expressed Aunt Lacey.

"Do you think one of the customers would buy it?" asked Sage.

"Place it on the shelf with the frames and night-lights."

Using both hands, Sage reached up and placed her picture beside a shiny blue frame. *Would anyone want her picture of shells? It would be just like being an artist,* thought Sage.

43

CHAPTER 10

The Customers

Sage heard the sound of the bell on the shop door. She turned to see who it was. A lady with two girls came into the shop. They went to the aisle where there were shelves filled with all types of seashells. Sage watched as the two girls looked through the different shells. They walked past the small treasure chest that Sage thought was so nice. The two girls stopped to look at the stuffed octopus, dolphins, and whales like Sam's. The taller girl pointed to the wooden shell picture Sage had just finished. "I like that picture," said the girl to her mother. "It would look nice in my room."

"Yes, I think it would," replied their mother as she reached for a book with a picture of a snail shell on the cover.

The other girl was younger. She had a little blond ponytail with a pink barrette. The little girl walked to the end of the aisle and stopped to look at the display of glittery glass fish ornaments. She reached out to touch one of the fish. Suddenly the little girl jumped back. "There's a cat in there!" she called out.

Sage hurried down the aisle to see what happened. Peeking through the display of hanging ornaments was Albert. He lifted his paw and pushed one of the dangling fish. It swung back and forth.

"Albert, what are you doing?" responded Sage as she gently stopped the ornament from moving. She did not want the ornament to drop off the hook and crash to the floor. Albert leaped off the end of the shelf without breaking anything. He was a big cat, but Albert knew how to get out of the tiniest places. They watched as he headed to the back of the shop. "Maybe the cat wanted to eat the fish," said the little girl.

"I think this book about seashells and fish will be interesting," said their mother. The little girl was searching through the bin of seashells. She selected three. "Let's go, girls," said their mother.

Sage went behind the checkout counter to help Aunt Lacey bag the items. She wrapped the picture carefully so the shells would not fall off.

"I hope you enjoy your picture," said Sage with a cheerful voice.

The little girl put one of the curved shells up to her ear.

"What do you hear?" asked Aunt Lacey.

The little girl looked up at her mother and back at Aunt Lacey. "Listen closely, and maybe you will hear the *message* of the seashell," replied Aunt Lacey.

Then the older girl spoke, "You must know a lot about seashells." Aunt Lacey nodded. "When I was a child, I collected seashells, and I read books about them. Now you can learn about seashells too."

When the group left the shop, Aunt Lacey turned and smiled. "You sold your first artwork." Sage felt really happy that someone liked her drawing. It was fun to make things that other people liked.

"Can I make more pictures?"

"You can make two pictures, and when they are sold, you can make two more," responded Aunt Lacey.

Sage was happy that she could make more pictures, but then she thought about the night before. She did not know what to say about the lights, the music, and the walking animals. How could she tell Aunt Lacey that she and Sam opened the door with the code and went into the shop? Why was all of that happening in the shop at night?

Sage walked toward the front of the shop to see Annie. She stopped for a moment to look at the little chest with the shell design sitting on the shelf at the end of the aisle.

The door of the shop opened. It was Mrs. Duffy and another lady that Sage did not know. "Good morning, ladies," greeted Aunt Lacey.

Sage turned and smiled. "Hello, Mrs. Duffy."

"This is my friend Emma," replied Mrs. Duffy. "She is visiting for a few days. Emma is looking for a gift for her granddaughter who is about your age." She looked at Sage, still standing at the end of the aisle.

"Sage, show the ladies the toys," said Aunt Lacey from the checkout counter.

Sage led the ladies to the aisle where the toys were located. Emma stopped and began to make motions with her hands and fingers to Mrs. Duffy. Mrs. Duffy did not speak. She used her hands the same way to her friend Emma. Sage remembered a girl in her classroom who was deaf. She used sign language, and it looked just like what Mrs. Duffy and Emma were doing. *When did Mrs. Duffy learn sign language? That is really neat that she knows sign language and can talk to her friend that way.*

Sage picked up the musical mermaid doll with the glittery green outfit. She pushed the button on the back of the toy, and the music started.

Why did I do that? Why did I turn on the music? If Emma can't hear, playing the music is not helpful. I want to help her find something for her granddaughter. She turned off the mermaid's song. Mrs. Duffy used sign language again. They moved down the aisle.

Sage pointed to the shiny fish ornaments and the seashell coloring books.

"Here are some nice bracelets," said Sage. The bracelets were hanging from a display rack. There were bracelets made with tiny shells and others with colorful beads. Sage slipped one of the bracelets on her wrist to show the ladies. As they walked to the end of the aisle, Sage stopped to show them the pretty chest with the pink shell design. It was her favorite thing in the shop.

The group went to the next aisle where the largest and most unusual seashells were displayed. Some were round and others were cone shaped. There were shells with spike shaped parts that looked like legs. These shells were home to sea creatures for many years, even decades. Sage learned a lot about seashells working in the shop with Aunt Lacey.

Emma looked across the row of fancy seashells. She reached up and selected a large conch shell with a beautiful pale-pink opening where the sea animal used to live. Emma turned toward Sage and lifted the palm of her hand up with her fingertips to her chin. She moved her hand back down and smiled. Sage did not know sign language, but she did understand that Emma was saying, "Thank you!"

Sage was happy that she was able to help Mrs. Duffy's friend Emma. Emma went to the checkout counter. "Thank you for your help, Sage. Seashells are a special treasure from the sea, and that's what Emma wanted," said Mrs. Duffy with a smile.

Now, there were no customers in the shop. Sage could hear Aunt Lacey talking on the phone. "Sounds good, I will send them back."

"It's your mother." She looked toward Sage from the checkout counter. "Your dad wants to go fishing."

"I will get Sam," replied Sage. Some customers were coming in the door as Sage quickly walked to the back of the shop.

Albert was curled up in the corner of a cardboard box. He appeared to be asleep. Sometimes, Albert looked like he was sleeping, but he was really very awake. Sam and Uncle Jonah were putting the sails on one of the ships.

"We have a lot of sails to put on this ship," said Sam as he turned to look at Sage from a tall stool at the large worktable. Just as Sage was ready to speak, there was a knock on the back door.

"Come in," called Uncle Jonah. The door opened, and a tall gray-haired man greeted them with a smile. He wore a brown hat, something like a cowboy would wear. He had a gold badge on a chocolate-colored shirt.

"Hi, guys," said the man.

"This is Sheriff Garcia. He is the sheriff of our town," said Uncle Jonah as he moved his head from behind the large white sails on the ship. "Sheriff Garcia, this is my niece, Sage, and my nephew, Sam. They are visiting the island and helping in the shop."

"Nice to meet you," said Sheriff Garcia. Sam pointed to Albert lying in the box. "That's our cat, Albert."

"Well, he looks like he found a comfortable bed in that box," said Sheriff Garcia with a friendly voice. Sage wanted to tell Sam that it was time to go, but she was not sure what to say.

Then Uncle Jonah spoke, "Is it time for you guys to go back to the cottage?"

"Dad wants us to go fishing," replied Sage in a soft voice.

"That sounds like fun," said Sheriff Garcia. Sam jumped down off the stool. Sheriff Garcia moved away from the opened door.

"Let's go fast. I'm hungry," said Sam.

CHAPTER 11

Going Fishing

"I can't wait to go fishing," said Sam as they walked up the steps to the porch door.

Sage could hear their mother talking. "Sage and Sam really enjoy helping at the shop."

"Jonah certainly builds some realistic ships," replied their father. They stopped talking when Sage and Sam came in the screen door.

"Come and have lunch," said their mother. After washing their hands, they went into the kitchen. Their mother was standing at the counter. "Here are your sandwiches." Each sandwich was on a bright-blue plate. The cabinets in the kitchen were filled with colorful plates and cups. Some were orange, others were a sunny yellow. "Your drinks are already on the table," said their mother as she pointed to the picnic table on the porch.

As Sage ate her sandwich, she thought about their day at the seashell shop. She thought about Mrs. Duffy and Emma. She thought about the pretty little treasure chest. Sage thought about going into the shop and seeing the toys moving and playing music. What should she do? She just did not know how to tell anyone.

Sam looked up from the other side of the table. "Here comes Uncle Jonah in his silver pickup truck." Their father came out on the porch. Uncle Jonah got out of the truck and called to Albert. "Come on, Albert." Albert jumped out of the truck and headed to the porch steps. Sam quickly got up to open the door. "I am going to pick up some supplies. Annie is still at the shop with Lacey, but I did not want to leave Albert in the back of the shop alone."

"Yes, I agree," replied their father.

"He might get into trouble," responded Sam in a concerned voice.

"Jonah, we are going fishing this afternoon, so when you are done, you can meet us at the pier," said their father.

"Okay, I hope you kids catch some fish for dinner," said Uncle Jonah as he looked toward Sam and Sage seated at the picnic table.

Albert took a drink from his water bowl in the corner of the porch. Then he jumped up on the green palm leaf cushion. He stretched out on the cushion with his eyes fixed on the porch door.

"Let's get ready to go," said their father.

"Yea!" Sam replied as he got up from the table.

"We can catch some fish for dinner," Sage echoing Uncle Jonah's words.

"I will leave the fishing up to you three. I'm going to help Aunt Lacey at the shop," said their mother from the kitchen.

Sam ran to their bedroom to get his ball cap with the anchor on it. Sage took her hat off the small wicker table. The table was beside the chair where Albert was lying. They always wore their hats when they went fishing. Their father gathered the fishing rods and tackle box sitting against the wall behind the picnic table.

"Bring your catch to Aunt Lacey's house. We are going to have dinner there tonight. Have fun fishing," said their mother.

"We will," replied their father. "Right, kids?" Sam and Sage nodded. "I want to get a really huge fish," said Sam with his arms stretched out wide.

A car drove into the driveway of the cottage next door. It stopped right behind the red golf cart. An older boy was driving the car, and a younger boy was with him. The younger boy did not look much older than Sage. Their father waved to the boys, and they smiled and waved back. The car was filled with bags of things, and two bikes were fastened to the rack on top.

"They live far away," said their father, reading the license plate on the back of the car. "Well, let's go fishing."

CHAPTER 12

The Search

"You are good fisherman. That was a great catch," said Aunt Lacey as she and Uncle Jonah stood at the door of their cottage.

"We'll see you tomorrow before you leave," expressed Uncle Jonah.

It was still light out, but it would be dark soon. The sound of the ocean grew louder as they walked toward the cottage. Annie stopped for a second when she heard a dog barking. It was Buddy from inside the Duffys' house.

"You all did a great job fishing," said their mother as they climbed the porch steps.

"We caught enough for a delicious dinner," their father replied.

"I caught the most fish," boasted Sam. Sage was too tired to respond. She went to put her hat back on the wicker table. There was Albert's favorite green palm leaf cushion, but the chair was empty. Albert was not there.

"Albert is not on his cushion," said Sage, bending down to look under the chair.

Their mother stopped at the kitchen door. She switched on the light and glanced around the porch. "I don't see him."

Their father was putting the fishing rods and tackle box back against the wall. He turned and quickly looked across the porch. "He's not out here."

"Albert, Albert," called Sam. Annie went over to Albert's cushion and sniffed. She turned her head and looked at the porch door and looked back again at the empty chair.

Sage, Sam, and their mother went inside and began to look around the cottage. They all called out for Albert as they went from room to room. Annie followed Sage as she looked under all the beds. Sam looked in every closet.

Their mother looked behind the large, brown leather sofa and chair. "I don't see him anywhere."

Their father came in the porch door. "I went outside and walked around the house, but there is no sign of him."

"Where can he be?" Cried Sam. He wiped his eyes with the back of his hand.

"Where did he go?" Sage replied as she and Annie came from the hallway.

"I think we should call Lacey and Jonah," said their mother, looking up as she searched behind the bags in the corner of the room.

"Yes, give them a call," replied their father. "I think we have looked everywhere around here."

"He must have gotten out of the cottage," said their mother. She went into the kitchen and came back with her phone.

Sage sat on the sofa, and Annie sat on the floor beside her. She reached down and placed her hand gently on Annie's head. "I hope we can find him," she said in a soft voice.

"It's getting dark outside," said Sam as he looked out of the glass doors leading to the deck.

Only a few minutes passed before Aunt Lacey and Uncle Jonah arrived.

"When we left to go fishing, Albert was sleeping on his chair," said their father.

"Albert never got lost before," replied their mother.

"Do you think he would go to the fishing pier?" asked Uncle Jonah. "I can head there and take a look."

"Good idea," replied their father. "I'll check the streets and down on the beach."

"I am going to go over to the Duffys' and ask them if they saw Albert," said their mother. "Mr. Duffy was sitting on the porch when I left for the shop this afternoon."

"I will take a look on Main Street," responded Aunt Lacey.

"Can we go with Aunt Lacey?" said Sage. Their mother looked at Aunt Lacey.

"Come on, both of you, and Annie too," replied Aunt Lacey with a grin. "We'll find him."

Their father went out the porch door first. He stopped when the older boy came out of the house next door. From the porch, Sage could hear her father talking. "Did you see a tabby colored cat?"

The boy came over to the driveway, and their father showed him a picture of Albert on his phone. Then Sage saw the boy take his keys from his pocket and get into the red golf cart. "I'll take a look around." He started the motor and drove out of the driveway.

That was nice of him to help look for Albert, Sage thought as she, Sam, and Annie walked with Aunt Lacey to the Main Street. Sage looked back and saw her mother crossing the road to the Duffys' house. "Maybe Mr. Duffy saw Albert," said Sage. "If you were Albert, where would you go?" asked Aunt Lacey.

They did not turn left toward the Treasure Chest Seashell Shop, but instead turned right onto Main Street. There were only a few stores opened. They passed Jim's Bakery, and the sign on the door said Closed. There were some people talking on the other side of the street.

A police car slowed down and stopped beside them. It was Sheriff Garcia. Aunt Lacey went over to the car. "We are looking for their cat. He is missing and was last seen at their cottage."

"I saw him at the shop this afternoon when I stopped in. I will keep a lookout for him. His name is Albert?"

"Yes, that's right," said Aunt Lacey. "And he is a very smart cat." Sheriff Garcia drove away.

"I hope we find him," said Sam.

Aunt Lacey took his hand. "Come on."

When they came to the end of the block, Aunt Lacey stopped. "Let's head back." They turned around and headed back toward the seashell shop. All the stores were closed now. Sage did not say anything. She looked on the steps of the shops, behind the parked cars, and under the bushes. There was no sign of Albert anywhere. Sam was sniffling, and Aunt Lacey gave him a tissue.

Aunt Lacey was reading a text on her phone.

"Did they find him?" asked Sage with an excited voice.

Aunt Lacey did not answer. The group of four started to walk faster. "We are going to meet everyone at the shop," Aunt Lacey replied. As they got closer, Sage could see her father talking to the boy in the red golf cart. Now she could see her mother appear under the streetlight. The group continued on Main Street until they arrived at the seashell shop.

"Thank you for looking for our cat," said their father to the boy in the red golf cart.

"No problem," replied the boy. "Our family lives on a farm, and we have lots of animals to care for. The farmer across the way had a broken fence, and lots of his steers got out. All the neighboring farmers stopped their work and went to look for them. Where I live, we always help our neighbor, and you're our neighbor. I hope you find your cat."

"Thanks again," said their father. The boy turned the golf cart around and headed back down the road to his cottage.

"He didn't find Albert. Tomorrow we are going home," said Sage. Her voice was almost a whisper. "How can we leave him on the island?"

"There is no sign of him," said their father.

"I talked to the Duffys," said their mother. "Mr. Duffy said he saw Albert looking through the porch screen around six o'clock when he was taking Buddy out for his walk."

Mystery in the Shop

Aunt Lacey walked to the front of the shop. "Where could he be?" Aunt Lacey did not finish speaking. She stopped and looked in the shop window. "What are those lights doing on?"

They all went to look. "Here comes the sheriff," said their father. Sheriff Garcia stopped his car. "Is everything okay?"

Sage, Sam, and Annie watched as Sheriff Garcia got out of his police car and walked to the window where Aunt Lacey was standing. "Did you find Albert yet?"

"No," responded Aunt Lacey. "There is something very strange going on in our shop."

"Let's take a look," said Sheriff Garcia.

Aunt Lacey put the code in, and with a quick turn of the knob, the door opened. She reached inside and turned on the lights. Sheriff Garcia went into the shop first. Sage could see Aunt Lacey and Sheriff Garcia walking up and down the aisles.

Sam stood on the step of the open door to get a good look inside. Sage moved as close to Annie as she could while watching from the sidewalk. Sage remembered what Uncle Jonah said about making

choices and prayer. She could see that all the toys were on. The light on the lighthouse was going around, and the musical mermaid was playing her song. There were crabs and turtles on the floor moving in every direction. It was just like the other night. The entire shop was filled with movement, sound, and lights.

Now Sage could hear Uncle Jonah's voice in the shop. "When I got to the back door it was open. The neat stack of empty boxes outside the back door were on the ground."

"Well, there is no one in here now," stated Sheriff Garcia.

Sam slowly stepped inside the open door. Then everyone came in and stood by the checkout counter. This time, Annie did not go to her favorite spot. She stood beside Sage. They watched as the toys moved with lots of action and lights. All of the toys were playing a different song at the same time.

"When I closed the shop today all of the toys were off and they were all on the shelves," said Aunt Lacey to Sheriff Garcia.

"This is unbelievable!" said their mother. "Who could have done this?"

Suddenly, there was a loud crash. Uncle Jonah quickly went to the corner of the shop, where he had built the new shelves. The large container that Sage had seen Uncle Jonah place on the top shelf was on the floor. Hundreds of seashells and colorful beads were dropping off the shelves and rolling across the floor and under the counters.

Sage looked up when she heard another sound. It was a scratching sound. There was one of Uncle Jonah's model ships rocking back and forth. Peeking out from behind its large sail was Albert.

"Don't move, Albert," their father called out. Uncle Jonah caught the ship just as it was about to fall. Albert looked down from the high shelf.

Quickly their mother spoke in a loud voice, "Don't jump, Albert!" Their father reached up, and Albert leaped in his arms.

"Now we know how this happened. Albert was able to get up on the stack of boxes at the back door," said Uncle Jonah.

"Yes, then he put the code in, and the door opened," replied their father.

"Can a cat do that?" asked Sheriff Garcia.

"Albert can," their father replied.

"Then he turned on all the toys," said their mother.

"That's amazing! Maybe Albert should work for the police force," responded Sheriff Garcia. "I just got a call, and everything is under control here." He turned and hurried out of the shop.

Albert jumped onto the floor and pushed some of the shells out of the way with his paw. Uncle Jonah went to the back room and brought out a large broom to push the shells into a pile. Everyone went to work, picking up the shells and beads. Aunt Lacey went around the shop, turning off all the toys. Sage put the walking crab and turtle back on their shelf. Now, Sage knew what happened in the shop the other night. This was not Albert's first time turning on the toys.

With everyone helping, the shop was cleaned up quickly. "Well, there was no harm done," expressed Uncle Jonah.

"Albert is a pretty amazing cat," replied Aunt Lacey.

"Yes, it is a big job for a cat to turn on all of these toys," their father replied.

"Sam, go sit on the floor and keep an eye on Albert," instructed their mother as she leaned down to pick up more shells. Sam sat on the floor with his arm around Albert. Sage could not wait any longer. This was her chance to tell everyone about going into the shop to get the whale. She looked at Sam, and the words came rushing out.

"This is not the first time that Albert came into the shop at night and turned on the toys. He did it before, and we saw it." Everyone stopped and looked at Sage as she spoke.

Sam looked up from his place on the floor. "I left my whale in the shop. I knew the code, so we could get in."

"I'm sorry," said Sage. She could hardly say the words, and her eyes filled with tears. Annie rubbed the side of her furry head on Sage's hand. "We shouldn't have gone in the shop. When we did, the toys were on and walking around."

"There were lots more toys on tonight," explained Sam, still sitting with Albert.

Uncle Jonah quickly spoke, "I think things look pretty good."

"Yes," agreed Aunt Lacey. "It's all cleaned up now."

Their father reached down and lifted Albert off the floor. "Let's go, kids." They all left the shop together. Aunt Lacey turned off the lights. Uncle Jonah was behind her closing the door.

"Wait!" called out Sage. "I see a light on inside." Sage went past Uncle Jonah and ran toward the light. It was the lighthouse. Its beacon of light danced from one wall to another. Her eyes followed the light as it moved. She reached up and pushed the switch off. Now it was dark inside the shop. Sage hurried outside, and Uncle Jonah closed the door.

As they walked toward the cottage, Sage could hear the sound of the waves. They were going home tomorrow. She would miss walking to the shop in the morning and seeing the old treasure chest in the window.

CHAPTER 14

The Message

At home, Sage sat in the velvet chair beside her bed. The seashells she found on Seabird Island were in a bag on her lap.

Sage was thinking about the mornings she spent helping in the seashell shop. She really liked helping Aunt Lacey.

The doll from Major Marsley was back on her bed. *I'm going to make a picture for Major Marsley. I can draw an astronaut, a spaceship, and the planet Mars.* Sage began to sort through the bag of seashells.

"You have a package, Sage," called her mother as she came in the front door, carrying two small boxes. Sage ran down the stairs and into the kitchen. Sam left his toys on the floor and ran to the counter. Annie followed Sam and stood beside him.

"They are from Aunt Lacey and Uncle Jonah," said their mother. "Here's yours, Sam, and this one is for you, Sage."

Sam pulled hard and tore off the tape and opened the box. He pushed back the paper surrounding the contents inside.

"Look! It's a boat like the ones Uncle Jonah makes. Just smaller," Sam responded with excitement. "There are even two sailors on the ship." Sam pointed to the tiny figures.

"That is really nice. Uncle Jonah said you were a great help building the ships," replied their mother.

Sage stood at the counter, looking at her package. *What could this be? I don't think it's a little boat like Sam's,* she thought. When she removed the lid, a smile appeared on her face. It was the treasure chest with the pink and white seashell design. It was the treasure chest she liked so much.

"How did Aunt Lacey know I liked this?" said Sage with a puzzled expression. She took the treasure chest out of the box and opened it. At once, she smelled the pleasant fragrance of the wood. The first thing she saw was a tiny gold key. Under the key was a paper. Sage placed the key on the counter and took the paper out of the chest. At the top of the paper in fancy print were the words "Treasure Chest Seashell Shop."

Below the fancy print, the *message* read, "As we grow on the outside, we want to grow on the inside."

"I remember Aunt Lacey's story about how seashells grow. She said it's something like people."

"Yes," replied their mother. "That is a valuable *message* to keep."

"I hope Aunt Lacey will trust me. I really like working in the shop. I am glad she did not get angry at us," said Sage as she looked at Sam still studying his model ship. She knew he was listening.

"I knew going in the shop at night was a bad idea. After we did it, I was afraid to tell anyone."

"As you grow up, it is good to stop and think before you do something. We are not like a robot or the toys in the seashell shop. We have a choice. We can choose to do what is right or wrong," said their mother. She paused and spoke again. "Truth brings our actions out of hiding and into the light."

"Uncle Jonah said a lighthouse keeps a ship away from danger," said Sam as he put the tiny sailor figures back on the ship.

Sage looked across the room where Albert was sitting.

"What is he doing?" asked Sage.

"He's watching a video about ship building," said Sam. "I can't wait to go back to Seabird Island."

"Me too," replied Sage, looking down at the paper in her hand. She put the *message* inside and closed the treasure chest.

ABOUT THE AUTHOR

 Shirley J. Lichty is a former teacher and early interventionist for children who are blind and vision impaired and those with developmental delays. As she worked with families, there was joy in seeing their child accomplish a milestone or perform a play activity. Shirley has been serving in adult and children's ministries in the local church she and her husband attend in Lancaster, Pennsylvania.

Shirley spent many family vacations with her children and grandchildren at Rehoboth Beach, Delaware, and Myrtle Beach, South Carolina. Searching for seashells and going to the local seashell shop was the inspiration for *Treasures in the Window*. We search for seashells, but what do we know about them? The ocean holds many treasures deep below the waves. What are our treasures? Shirley brings together imagination, life experiences, and biblical truths for children to understand and treasure.